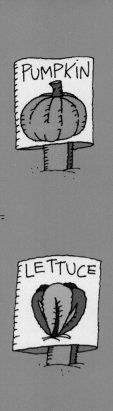

This Book Belongs to:

_____

Name

For Lawrence, Sueanne and Stacie
whose sense of wonder inspired
this garden book
back in 1969.

 The Giggles Group

ISBN: 1-892780-03-8

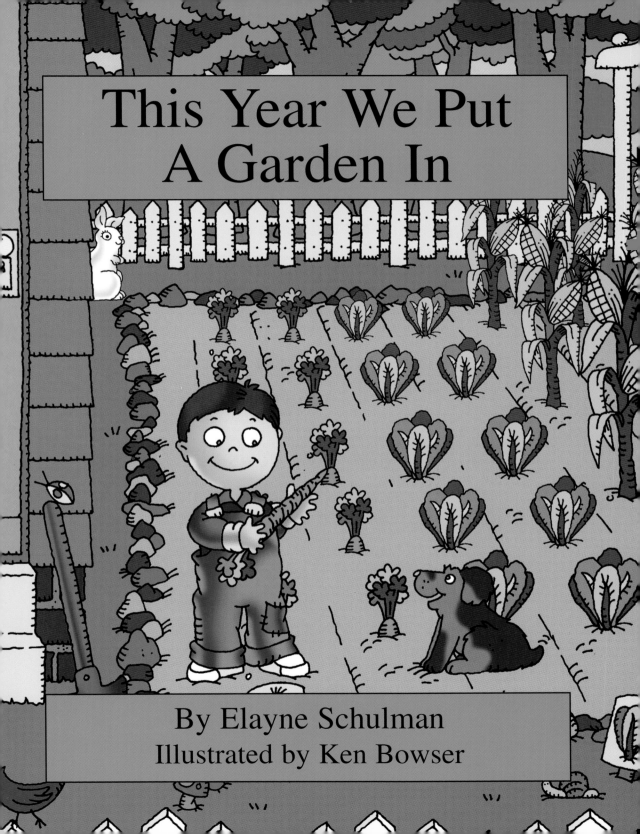

This Year We Put A Garden In

By Elayne Schulman

Illustrated by Ken Bowser

This year we put a garden in
Right near the kitchen door.
Dad turned the earth; Mom bought the seeds.
They cleared the ground and more!

I helped to make the rows all straight,
As neat as they could be.
Dad marked a special little piece,
And gave it just to me.

The seeds went in each narrow row,
So tiny they did look.
They didn't seem at all like things
That we would want to cook!

I couldn't tell the lettuce from
The radish, beans or peas,
All in the ground and covered up
As fast as you could please.

And all the while just watching us,
A bunny waiting near.
What could she want, that silly thing,
Waiting, watching, over there?

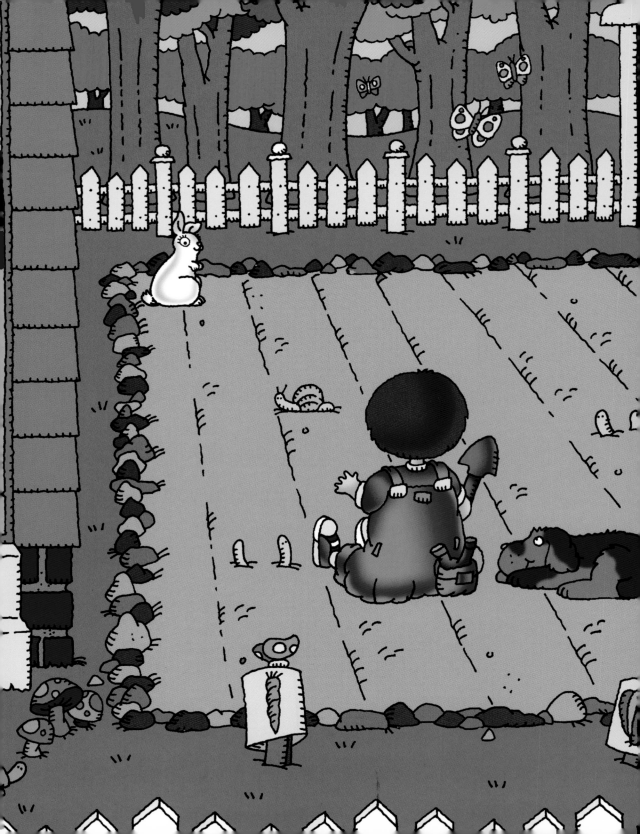

Each day I looked to see what grew
Before I went to play.
I looked as hard as I could look
But nothing came that day!

We watered all the garden space
Just so a seed would sprout.
I thought we'd made some big mistake.
"Come up!" I'd want to shout.

One morning I'd just given up
When Mom came in to say,
"Go out and check the garden space
And see what's up today."

I raced out back; my sneakers flew,
As fast as they could go.
And there I saw the garden up,
Each tiny, neat, green row.

And all the while just watching us
A bunny waiting near.
What could she want, that silly thing,
Waiting, watching, over there?

In time we had the joy of it -
Lettuce, carrots, and peas.
Tomatoes picked and eaten warm,
Corn stalks as big as trees.

We had to search all through the earth
To seek a hidden treat,
Potatoes deep beneath the top
Waiting for us to eat.

We picked the summer crook-necked squash,
(A funny sounding name)
For something tasting oh, so good
It made me leave my game.

I found some leafy carrot tops
And pulled them up so straight
Revealing long thin treasures there
Which turned up on my plate.

And all the while just watching us.
A bunny waiting near.
What could she want, that silly thing,
Waiting, watching, over there?

One morning though, the bunny's gone,
Not in her usual spot.
I hunted under all the shrubs,
Then near the garden plot.

Now tears and tears came to my eyes,
She wasn't any place!
I searched and cried until I fell
Down in the garden space.

A strange noise, a quiet sound
Came from the middle row.
I looked up through my dripping tears
To see a wondrous show.

The bunny sitting midst my plants
Wide-eyed, her ears up high,
Nibbling lettuce, carrots and peas.
Oh my! Oh my! Oh my!

The garden's done, but bunny's there
Our bunny waiting near
She will be back, no silly thing
Waiting, watching, for next year.

Garden Glossary

 bunny

 butterfly

 carrot

 corn

 cornstalk

 frog

 grasshopper

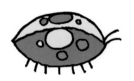 ladybug

 lettuce

 mushroom

 peas

 potato

 pumpkin

 rocks

seeds

 snail

 squash

 tomato

 worm